The Old, Old Man and
the Very Little Boy

The Old, Old Man and the Very Little Boy

BY KRISTINE L. FRANKLIN
ILLUSTRATED BY TEREA D. SHAFFER

ATHENEUM • 1992 • NEW YORK

Maxwell Macmillan Canada
Toronto

Maxwell Macmillan International
New York Oxford Singapore Sydney

Atheneum
Macmillan Publishing Company
866 Third Avenue
New York, NY 10022

Maxwell Macmillan Canada, Inc.
1200 Eglinton Avenue East
Suite 200
Don Mills, Ontario M3C 3N1

Macmillan Publishing Company is part of the Maxwell Communication Group of Companies.

First edition

Printed in Hong Kong

10 9 8 7 6 5 4 3 2 1

The text of this book is set in Trump Medieval.

The illustrations are rendered in oil paints.

Library of Congress Cataloging-in-Publication Data

Franklin, Kristine L.
    The old, old man and the very little boy/by Kristine L. Franklin;
    illustrated by Terea D. Shaffer.—1st ed.
        p.   cm.
    Summary: As he listens to Old Father's stories each day, a little
boy asks if his friend has ever been young, but only after he has
grown old himself does he understand Old Father's answer.
    ISBN 0-689-31735-2
    [1. Old age—Fiction.]   I. Shaffer, Terea D., ill.   II. Title.
PZ7.F85922601   1992
[E]—dc20   91-26211

To my dear husband, Marty
K. L. F.

To my family and Richard Rosenblum
T. D. S.

Once there was an old, old man. His hair was the color of the clouds. His face was wrinkled and as brown as the deep garden soil. His feet were tough and wide, and his old toes spread like stubby fingers because he had always walked barefoot wherever he went.

Each morning, when the sun made enough light to warm his bones, the old, old man sat on a stump and waited. The women of the village passed him on their way to dig in the gardens.

"Will the rains come soon, Old Father?" asked a young woman in a loud voice. The old, old man closed his eyes and nodded wisely.

"Soon it will rain!" shouted the women with great smiles. They walked down the trail, singing about sunshine and rain and all the things that make life good.

The young men gathered to sharpen their spears. They chanted magic spells and sang hunting songs, and though the old, old man knew all of the spells and all of the songs, he kept silent.

"Will we find food, Old Father?" asked one young man. The old, old man closed his eyes and nodded wisely.

"Full bellies tonight!" shouted the young men. They left for the forest, singing about sharp spears and roasted meat and all the things that make life good.

"Good morning, Old Father," said a bright little voice. To the old, old man it sounded like the twittering of a bird. "Good *morning, Old Father,*" said the voice a little louder. And the old, old man knew who it was. It was a very little boy who came to sit with him every day. "Mother sent this," said the boy as he unfolded a banana leaf. Inside was a roasted sweet potato.

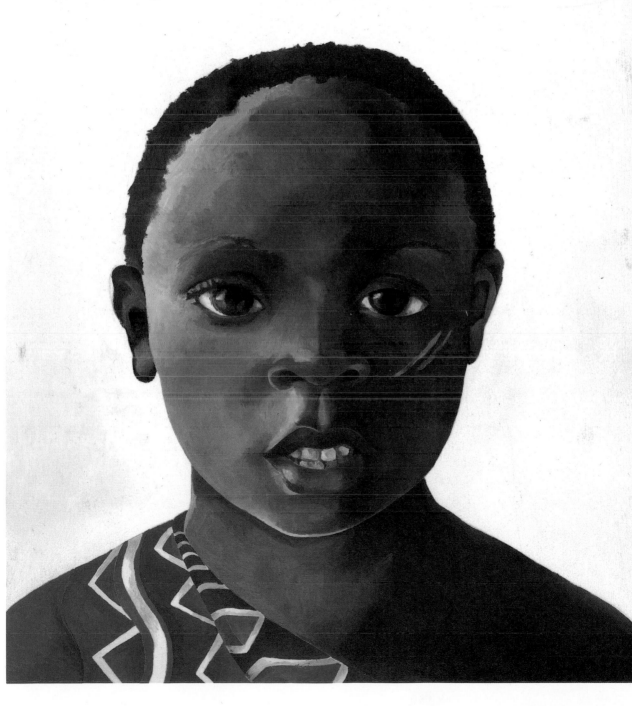

The old, old man ate the potato slowly. Most of his teeth were gone. He licked his fingers one by one and politely smacked his lips when he was done. Each day began like this.

"Tell me a story," the little boy begged in a loud voice, for the old, old man could scarcely hear. The old, old man smiled a wide, toothless grin and closed his eyes.

"When I was young and proud . . . ," he always began, and his voice was as dry as the dust. He told the same tales again and again, but the little boy never grew tired of them. The old, old man told stories of hunting and bravery and the sweetness of love. The little boy danced in the dirt before him.

"Aaaaaaaah-ya! yip! yip! yip!" he yelled as he whirled and hopped and threw sticks at a tree. The old, old man smiled sweetly and remembered many things.

"Were you ever a little boy, Old Father?" the little boy asked one day. The old, old man laughed a crackly laugh.

"Come close," he whispered. The little boy leaned over and listened. The old, old man thumped his chest with a leathery fist. "Inside this old, old man," he said, "lives a very little boy."

The little boy laughed and laughed. It was the funniest thing he had ever heard. The old, old man laughed too, until one silver tear trickled down his wrinkled cheek.

Soon the sun plunged toward the western horizon and the little boy's mother came for him. "Good night, Old Father," said the little boy. "Tomorrow we will laugh again."

"Tomorrow," said the old, old man, "you will be too old to sit with me." The little boy laughed as he walked down the trail with his mother. He knew he would never be old.

Around and around the seasons danced. Wet and dry, wet and dry. The old, old man and the very little boy laughed and sang and chanted magic spells together, and the boy grew like a banana tree.

Then one day the boy's father gave him a spear of his very own. "Today you will hunt with the men," said his father.

"See my beautiful spear!" shouted the boy as he passed the old, old man on the way to the forest. The old, old man smiled and nodded wisely.

From that time on, the boy saw his friend every morning before the hunt, but he did not sit with the old, old man again.

One gray, rainy day the old, old man died and rested with the others who had died before him.

At first the boy missed the old, old man, but the seasons chased each other as they always had and he forgot his friend. The boy learned to throw a spear and shoot an arrow. Soon he was a young man.

The young man hunted and danced with the other young men and told stories by the fire each night. When it was time to take a wife, he chose the finest girl in the village to be his bride.

The seasons changed twice and their first child was born. Then many seasons passed and there were many children, and the man was proud and brave and his life was good.

Many more years passed, and one day the man left the hunting
to the younger men, for he wanted only to sit on the old stump and
warm himself in the sun. Soon the little boys gathered at his feet.

"A story, Old Father, a story!" the littlest boy cried. And the old man placed the boy on the stump beside him.

"When I was young and proud . . . ," he began. And the boys were quiet and the smooth breeze carried his old voice across the village as he told tales of hunts and battles, and sang songs of bravery and love.

"Were you ever a little boy?" asked the littlest boy. The old man chuckled and coughed and slapped his bare legs with both hands.

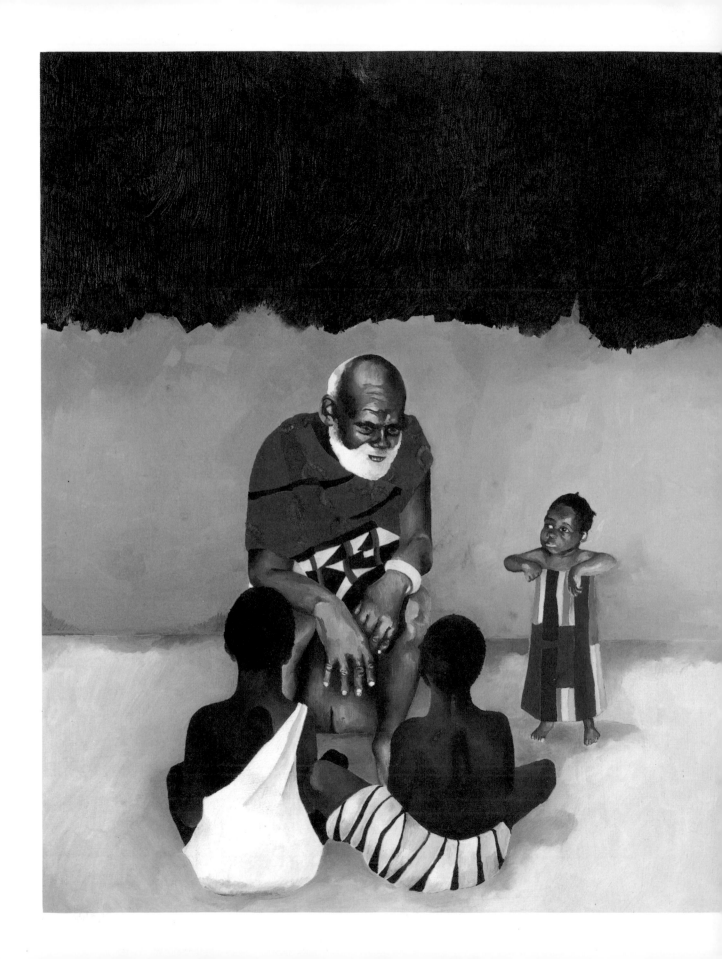

"I will tell you a secret," he whispered, and the
little boys gathered near to listen. "Inside this old,
old man is a very little boy."

The boys laughed and laughed. Their mouths
were wide open with joy.

"You were old yesterday and the day before and
the day before," said one of the little boys. "You are
the oldest man we know."

"We see your wrinkled face!" said one boy.

"We see your rough hands!" said another boy.

"We see your wide feet!" said another.

"You have been old for a long time," said the
littlest boy. "You have been old forever."

The old, old man grinned a toothless grin and shook his finger at the boys. "Tomorrow," he said, "you will understand. Tomorrow you will be old men just like me."

The little boys laughed and laughed as they danced in the dirt before him. They knew they would never be old.

The old, old man laughed too, until one silver tear trickled down his wrinkled cheek. With a crooked finger, he wiped away the tear and smiled, and remembered many things.

Deep within his old, old heart, a very little boy was dancing in the dirt.